FREE GIFT

* * * * * * * *

Thank you so much for your support. I am extending a free 15-minute purpose planning session to everyone who has purchased this book.

Discovering your purpose will change your life and give you a launching pad for your destiny. Whether you are fifteen or forty-five, it's never too late to pursue your dreams.

If you want to brainstorm with me about moving your life forward, visit my website at adriennemayfield.com, and book a free 15-minute consultation using the code "BURNING BUSH."

I'M TIRED OF THIS CHURCH

LOSING RELIGION TO FIND GOD

Adrienne Mayfield, Esq.

BURNING BUSH
BOOKS

I'm Tired Of This Church: Losing Religion To Find God

Published by Burning Bush Books

Copyright © 2019 by Adrienne Mayfield

All rights reserved

First edition: June 2019

For information about bulk purchases, please contact Adrienne Mayfield at amayfield2147@gmail.com.

Manufactured in the United States of America

ISBN: 978-0-9997694-5-4

All Scripture quotations, unless otherwise noted, were taken from the Holy Bible, New King James Version (NKJV).

Cover Design: Adrienne Mayfield

Cover Image: Desy Suryani

Visit the author's website at adriennemayfield.com

This book is dedicated to every person who feels lost and misunderstood

TABLE OF CONTENTS

ACKNOWLEDGMENTS

Thank you, Father, for your tireless and faithful commitment to me. I am forever humbled and honored that you would choose to give me the opportunity to speak life to your people. Because of your love for me, I will finish my race with perseverance and grace.

And when I passed by you and saw you struggling in your own blood, I said to you in your blood, 'Live!' Yes, I said to you in your blood, 'Live!'

Ezekiel 16:6

INTRODUCTION

In Herman Maslow's paper, "A Theory of Human Motivation," he discusses five stages that human beings travel through on their way to self-fulfillment. After the first stage, which entails basic needs such as food, water, warmth, and rest, the next stage is the need for security and safety. Within each individual is an innate desire to be known and accepted unconditionally. People seek to find these things in many different places, but for many, religion becomes the answer.

I was raised in church, and I was always taught that being a good person was a natural occurrence of being a Christian, yet I often encountered many people who were far from "good." Even as a child, I noticed a huge divide between what people in church said they believed and what I saw them live out in practice.

At times, I became disgruntled, and my discontent actually led me on a journey to discover if there was something more. In my heart, I had always hoped and prayed, but I just wasn't sure. I had so many questions that were not addressed, and the God people talked about seemed untouchable and disconnected. Through a very difficult period in my life, I turned toward the church and the people there to heal my wounded soul. When they were unable to heal me, I concluded that I was "tired of church." In actuality, God was showing me that religion had nothing to offer me. He began to reveal that He was actually the lover of my soul and the one who could offer me the healing I sought. He invited me to take a journey of exploration to discover Him, His nature, and His purpose for my life. He invites you to take this same journey with Him today. Join me as you discover how to lose your religion, so you can find God. Before you begin, please pray this prayer out loud with me.

Father, I thank you that you have chosen this moment in time for me to learn more about you and how you see me. Open my heart, my mind, and my soul to the Truth you want me to receive. May this book not merely be words on a page, but answers to questions and healing for my soul. Amen.

CHAPTER 1

WE ARE OFFERED RELATIONSHIP NOT RELIGION

One of the myths about having a relationship with God is that there are too many rules to follow. Nothing could be further from the truth. In actuality, having a relationship with God is actually about approaching Him in faith—no masks, no hiding, no shame. You can come to Him just as you are. Religion is about pretense and rules, but relationship is about intimacy, acceptance, and understanding.

In Matthew 23, Jesus actually challenged the religious leaders of that day because of their emphasis on their outside appearance and reputation, while neglecting the weightier issues of the heart. As Jesus taught the multitudes, he encouraged them to observe the things the religious leaders told them to observe but not to follow their works. His reasoning was blunt and to the point. "They do not do according to their works; for they say and do not do." V. 3. We must avoid this dangerous trap of the religious—we must not say and pretend to be one thing when in actuality we are doing something else.

Jesus' next challenge to them concerns the heavy burden of perfection the leaders place on others. The religious leaders wanted people to believe that God was keeping score, and they were always losing or behind. In doing so, "they bind heavy burdens, hard to bear, and lay *them* on men's shoulders; but they themselves will not move them with one of their fingers." V.4. They created insurmountable obstacles to get to God—obstacles that God, himself, had not even intended. They made it virtually impossible to get to God by their expectations but were willing to do nothing to help others understand how to actually have a relationship with God.

Today the religious spirit functions in much the same way. Just when we think we are okay, it adds another requirement. If we pray for 15 minutes, it makes us think we should feel guilty for not praying for 30. If we fall asleep while reading our Bible, it accuses us of not really loving God. The system of trying to achieve check marks never stops.

Jesus further challenged the leaders because "all their works they do to be seen by men. They make their phylacteries broad and enlarge the borders of their garments." V. 5. Nothing they

4

did was because of their genuine love for God. Their actions and perceived devotion was only so it would be observed by men. Phylacteries are boxes that contain verses of the Torah that the religious leaders wore when they prayed. The borders of their garments were also widened to be an outward show of their superiority as religious leaders. They believed that religious activities and clothes established them as God's people.

Religion has not changed much today. Many people believe that they get brownie points for things like going to church, doing a five-minute devotional, and praying over their food. Some people in church still argue over whether women should be allowed to wear pants. None of those things prove that you have a relationship with God. We have to guard against this dangerous trap of religion. Jesus' rebuke makes it clear. God's primary concern is with the condition of our hearts.

Jesus' primary message and life emphasized humility. He encouraged the disciples to prefer others over themselves. The Pharisees and Scribes were the exact opposite. "They love the best places at feasts, the best seats in the synagogues, greetings in the marketplace, and to be called, Rabbi, Rabbi. . . He who is greatest among you shall be your servant. And whoever exalts himself will be humbled, and he who humbles himself will be exalted." V. 6-7; 11-12.

The leaders wanted everyone to reverence their position as religious leaders. They wanted front row seats at events, to be revered when they were out in public, and referred to by their titles. Many times, modern religion mimics that of Jesus' day. The front row and "VIP seating" are reserved for spiritual leaders. I've always thought it actually made more sense for visitors and those that we are leading to Christ to sit in front. Whenever I sit at the back of a church, I usually observe cell phones, tablets, and snacking children. Maybe some of those people might be more engaged if they were "allowed" to sit in one of the "special" seats. In reference to titles, I believe in honoring leaders and respecting their natural and spiritual authority, but sometimes things can go too far.

Once I traveled to minister with several believers. There were apostles, pastors, ministers, teachers, evangelists on the trip. I accidentally referred to one of the Apostles by her first name, and she sternly corrected me. I apologized profusely, assuring her I meant no offense. She didn't seem convinced, but she kept walking. A few days later, we were on the same ministry team. She ministered first, and I followed. After I finished, we fellowshipped with some of the ladies until it was time for the next station. When it was time to go, we headed toward the door, and one of the women called for me. As I looked back, I noticed that my teammate, "the Apostle," had left her Bible. I went back to get it

6

and walked up to catch her. I called her by her first name (oops) and said, "You almost left your Bible." She snatched it from my hand, grimaced, and said, "I TOLD YOU NOT TO CALL ME BY MY FIRST NAME!" Her response made me think I should have just left her Bible. This story perfectly illustrates what Jesus was talking about.

Everything that Jesus came to Earth to do was about restoring our access to the Father. Thus, as he watched the Pharisees and scribes restrict access to God, He issued an additional rebuke, "But woe to you, scribes and Pharisees, hypocrites! For you shut up the kingdom of heaven against men; for you neither go in yourselves, nor do you allow those who are entering to go in." v.13. Jesus challenged the tendency of the leaders to convince people that they are unworthy to have access to the kingdom of God while refusing the relationship with God that they pretended to have. Religion creates a hierarchy where those who desire to know God are prevented to do so if they do not measure up to the religious leaders' standards. There is no doubt that many people have left the modern church for this very reason.

Certain denominations create intermediaries that ask that you pray to them in order to get to God. Religion attempts to create barriers, so people focus on programs more than the person of Jesus Christ. While it is right and helpful to pray with others and even ask other people to pray for us, Christ alone provides access to the Father. "For there is one God and one Mediator between God and men, the Man Christ Jesus, who gave Himself a ransom for all, to be testified in due time. . ." 1 Timothy 2:5-6.

Jesus died so that we can have access to Him. When he trained His disciples, he emphasized that His purpose was to reveal the Father. His blood was shed so that we could re-enter a right relationship with God. The Pharisees and scribes went to great lengths to train individuals in keeping the law, thereby leaving them in a worse state than before. "Woe to you, scribes and Pharisees, hypocrites! For you travel land and sea to win one proselyte, and when he is won, you make him twice as much a son of hell as yourselves." V. 15. Stories of abuse in the Catholic church and beyond are examples of this travesty. When people come to church seeking wholeness and leave more broken, something is terribly wrong. No one should ever be 8umin8le into darkness in their quest for God.

Jesus loves people. We are created in God's image, and we are the apple of His eye. Just in case you doubt that fact, Zechariah records it in chapter 2, verse 8. "For thus says the LORD of hosts: He sent Me after glory, to the nations which plunder you; for he who touches you touches the apple of His eye." God sees every life as valuable, and He desires that we love each other just as He

8

has loved us. When injustice and hate abound, I know the heart of God is grieved.

Jesus exhorted the Pharisees for this inconsistency in verse 23 of Matthew 23. "Woe to you, scribes and Pharisees, hypocrites! For you pay tithe of mint and anise and 9 umin, and have neglected the weightier *matters* of the law: justice and mercy and faith. These you ought to have done, without leaving the others undone." They took pride in paying their monetary dues, yet left their responsibility to people unaddressed. Jesus rebukes them for neglecting the weightier matters of the law, which he established as justice, mercy, and faith.

One issue in modern culture immediately comes to mind. Some people who refer to themselves as Christians would say they have a strict pro-life stance; yet, those same individuals often don't support the healthcare necessary for the children once they are here. Those individuals also often are proponents of the death penalty. The inconsistency stands to question—At what point does life become valuable? It's definitely something to think about.

We must not be like Dr. Jekyll and Mr. Hyde. When people encounter us, they shouldn't have to wonder which person they will get. Our public and private face should be the same. Otherwise, we are just hypocrites. Jesus challenged the Pharisees on this very issue in verses 25-27. "Woe to you, scribes and Pharisees, hypocrites! For you cleanse the outside of the cup and dish, but inside, they are full of extortion and self-indulgence. Blind Pharisee, first cleanse the inside of the cup and dish, that the outside of them may be clean also." They put all their emphasis on their reputation with men. Though they worked hard to follow all the rules, Jesus launched a powerful rebuke. All their focus was on external things. They used their perceived piety as a way to elevate themselves above others. Yet, when Jesus evaluated their hearts, they were full of the things they judged to disqualify others.

Their attempts at doing all the right things were from an impure motive. It was not their love for God that motivated them, but their desire to be seen and worshipped by men. Religion would have us be in bondage to a false relationship with God so that we never pursue an authentic relationship with Him. If we accept the counterfeit, we will be trapped in a cycle of performance that we will never escape. When, not if, we fail to perform properly, we will begin to feel the pressure to feel worthless or hide the reality of our fall.

Feeling like we have to hide from God is actually a trick of the enemy. It goes all the way back to the Garden of Eden, where Adam and Eve enjoyed daily communion with God. Scripture tells us that God came to them in the cool of the day and talked with them. I imagine the song, "In The Garden," by C. Austin Miles adequately describes what life for Adam and Eve was like.

I come to the garden alone

While the dew is still on the roses

And the voice I hear falling on my ear

The Son of God discloses.

And He walks with me, and He talks with me,

And He tells me I am His own;

And the joy we share as we tarry there,

None other has ever known.

Adam and Eve enjoyed unfiltered, unmasked intimacy with God. They knew God, and they were known by Him. All that changed when the snake deceived Eve into thinking that God was withholding something from her. Once she believed the lie and disobeyed God's command, the Bible says she and Adam immediately were naked and ashamed. Instinctively, they knew something major had shifted in their position with God. So when he came to speak with them that day, they hid themselves.

We have been hiding ever since—afraid to be open and exposed to a God, who ironically knows all about us anyway. God knows our hearts, and he knows us much better than we know ourselves. He is omniscient, which means that there is nothing He does not know. Quiet yourself. Let that sink in. He already knows you completely, and He still chooses to have a relationship with you. That fact should be very freeing because that means nothing you have ever done surprises God. In fact, since He is all-knowing, He actually could never be surprised. It follows that He likely could not be disappointed, either, since disappointment comes when some expectation is not met. Since He already knows all outcomes, He never has reason to expect that something different will occur. God, Himself said it in Jeremiah 31:3. **"Yes, I have loved you with an everlasting love; Therefore, with lovingkindness I have drawn you."** Breathe that in. The God that we hide from, fearing judgement for our mistakes actually wants to meet with us. He longs to meet with you, to be known by you and to enjoy a fellowship of intimacy and oneness with you. That means you must be pretty special! Please pray this prayer out loud with me.

Father, I thank you for the gift of authentic relationship with you through Jesus Christ. Today, I choose to take off my fig leaves. I won't hide from you anymore. You desire truth in my inward parts, so I will open my heart, my mind, and my soul to you. I invite you to destroy every false lie I have embraced about who you are and how you see me. I decree that I am loved by you. I am accepted by you. You will never turn me away. Thank you for your unconditional acceptance of me. I accept your invitation to know you and be known by you. Thank you for your love. Amen.

CHAPTER 2

WE BECOME SONS NOT SLAVES

If someone asked you if you are a slave, you'd probably be offended, yet the truth is, if you are controlled by someone or something, you could potentially become a slave. A slave is defined as a person who is the legal property of another and is forced to obey them. Most would argue that there is no way they are enslaved, yet some people feel powerless to make decisions that advance their lives.

To get further insight, let's take a closer look at how the crisis in the Garden of Eden began. "The LORD God planted a garden eastward in Eden, and there He put the man whom He had formed. And out of the ground the LORD God made every tree grow that is pleasant to the sight and good for food. The tree of life was also in the midst of the garden, and the tree of the knowledge of good and evil." Genesis 2:8-9. God created a beautiful garden and put the man inside for its maintenance. With

14

this responsibility came one simple instruction and an accompanying warning. And the Lord God commanded the man, saying, "Of every tree of the garden you may freely eat; but of the tree of the knowledge of good and evil, you shall not eat, for in the day that you eat of it you shall surely die." V. 16-17.

Soon after, God created Eve as Adam's helper and they lived in paradise. One day, a stranger approached Eve. He was not just any stranger. He engaged Eve with a specific agenda. He sought to destroy the relationship she enjoyed with God. To accomplish his objective, he enticed her to question the goodness of God. "Now the serpent was more cunning than any beast of the field which the LORD God had made. And he said to the woman, 'Has God indeed said, 'You shall not eat of every tree of the garden?'" v. 3. Eve made a very destructive decision—she entertained conversation with the enemy. She repeated the admonition God had given them about the tree. "We may eat the fruit of the trees of the garden; but of the fruit of the tree which is in the midst of the garden, God has said, 'You shall not eat it, nor shall you touch it, lest you die.'" V. 2-3.

Her response made it all clear. She knew the rules. She knew what God said, yet she allowed the serpent to speak further. "Then the serpent said to the woman, 'You will not surely die. For God knows that in the day you eat of it your eyes will be opened,

15

and you will be like God, knowing good and evil.'" V. 4-5. One word inserted wouldn't change much, right? Wrong. Eve fell for the deception. She accepted the lie that God was attempting to withhold something from her. She bought into the false belief that God really didn't know what was best for her. "So when the woman saw that the tree was good for food, that it was pleasant to the eyes, and a tree desirable to make one wise, she took of its fruit and ate. She also gave to her husband with her, and he ate." V.6.

When Adam and Eve sinned in the garden, everything about their world shifted. In their rebellion against God, they believed the lie that their desires and beliefs were superior to God's. Ever since their decision, man has been born with a bent away from God. We fight with all in our being to be in control. As a matter of fact, several years ago, one of the common slogans was, "You're not the boss of me." Something inside of us clamors to be our own boss, call the shots and run the show. This desire for autonomy has proved to be more of a curse than blessing.

We foolishly demand independence from the Creator, only to discover that in our "freedom," we become slaves. Without a moral compass and submission to God, we become victims of our sin nature. We make series of bad choices that land us in destructive cycles of pain and despair. In the beginning, we make the choices, but in short order, the decisions begin to control us, and we become slaves—slaves to our desires and powerless to resist the very things that are leading to our demise.

Consider someone who is addicted to drugs. In most cases, it starts as recreational activity, often just for fun. As experimentation continues, addiction ensues. Suddenly, the one who chose to use the drug becomes its slave. Use is no longer a choice; the body develops a dependency on its effects that the individual cannot resist. Once freedom of choice ends; slavery ensues. Countless people have watched hopelessly as their financial security, family, and hope turns to ashes.

Slaves work with no guaranteed benefit. They have an expectation of punishment or rejection when they fail. They do not get an inheritance. They can't approach their master unless they are summoned. Before we accept Jesus, we are slaves to sin. We are bound to a cycle that leads to destruction and death. Through a relationship with Jesus, we are given an offer to be accepted unconditionally in the arms of a Father who knows us completely. Accepting the offer positions us as sons. We become heirs of God and joint-heirs with Christ. We are no longer separated from His love; we are not rejected because of our past mistakes. In Ephesians 1:6, Paul tells us that because of the blood of Jesus Christ, we are" accepted in the Beloved." We have an

17

inheritance of abundant life here and in heaven when we die. Better still, we can approach His throne boldly with confidence and make requests to Him, being assured that He hears us. Hebrews 4:16. Religious activity and trying to do everything right doesn't guarantee us this access to God; it is only made possible because of the blood of Jesus Christ.

The tabernacle was a depiction of the Throne Room of Heaven. The central image of the holiest of holies is the mercy seat. The blood was spilled from a sacrificial animal to cover the sins of the people. Once a year, the priest entered to place the blood there to satisfy the requirement of blood for propitiation, or payment, for sin. Jesus came and lived a sinless life; he died to pay for our sins once and for all. Now his blood, still spilled on the mercy seat in Heaven, grants us access to the throne of the Father. His blood means that we can approach God naked and unashamed. That means we are accepted.

Romans 8:14 says, "For as many as are led by the Spirit of God, these are the sons of God." Being a son of God is not gender-specific. Son is a relational term. When we accept Jesus, we become God's children. "For you did not receive the spirit of bondage again to fear, but you received the Spirit of adoption by whom we cry out, 'Abba, Father.'" Roman 8:15. The term "Abba" is the English equivalent to Daddy. We become part of God's family where we are valued, accepted, recognized, and redeemed. We can approach God and expect to be welcomed and accepted into His Presence without fear.

In Roman culture a child born into a family could be disinherited, such was not the case for one who was adopted. Someone adopted could NEVER be disinherited. That is amazing news for us since we are "adopted" or grafted into the family of God. God will never throw us away or pretend we do not belong to Him. Many people who read the last sentence will find tension between their experience and acceptance of that statement. We live in a fallen world where the family structure is often fractured. Some may not even have met their father. Others may only know their father as absent, abusive, or dysfunctional. I caution you not to let whatever your experience has been to cloud your view of your Heavenly Father. He is dependable. He is consistent. He is faithful, and He loves you. Your ability to reconcile that belief in your heart is central to living your life as a son rather than a slave. As a son of God, you can talk to Him, spend time with Him, know Him, and hear His voice. Please pray this prayer out loud with me.

Father, for far too long I have lived my life as a slave. I have lived beneath my rights and privileges as a (son/daughter) of the Most High God. I am an heir of God and a joint heir with Christ. Nothing can stop me. Anything that has tried to enslave me or keep me in bondage, I renounce now. I come out of agreement with it and command it to go. Thank you for accepting me into your family. I am not a slave. I walk in the Spirit of Adoption. Help me learn to just accept your love without trying to earn it or work for it. It is for freedom that Christ has set me free. I will stand firm and not allow myself to live like a slave again. Amen.

CHAPTER 3

WE ARE VICTORIOUS NOT DEFEATED

We are a very competitive people. In America, we take our sports competitions seriously. As a matter of fact, in the movie, "Concussion," when the main character questions why the NFL is coming after him, his colleague tells him, "The NFL owns a day of the week—the same day the church used to own." That statement alone points to our perceived obsession with sports, which can have very dangerous repercussions. From birth, parents groom their children for the moment when they can stand proudly on the sidelines, and shout, "That's my baby! That's my boy! That's my girl!" While it might seem innocent, often, this desire for winning is passed on to our children in an unhealthy way.

An obsession with winning follows us into adulthood. It lands us on a hamster wheel, striving for external success, acceptance, and notoriety. If you add religion with its emphasis on punishment and shame when you fail, people are left feeling hopeless and worthless. Having a fixation with being perfect and never making a mistake likens itself to the proverbial cookie jar or cooling brownies on the stove. Once someone identifies them as off-limits, it is the only thing we can think about. Once we succumb to the temptation, we instantly feel the accompanying shame. We can also become burdened with shame when we believe we failed to meet others' expectations of us.

One common characteristic of those who are religious is repetitive cycles of behavior. They keep doing the same thing over and over without any lasting change. Despite the most valiant efforts to be "perfect" and please God, their efforts fail. They may, at times be able to meet societal standards, but those of a holy God far outweigh them. Therefore, they cower away in shame whenever they are unsuccessful.

This has been the plight of man from the very beginning. Before Adam and Eve sinned, they enjoyed the fellowship with God. After they fell, they immediately realized that something had changed. The chasm that appeared in their ability to commune with God was immediate. When God came to speak with them as He always had, they hid themselves. They knew they had failed. They knew they had disappointed God, and they knew there would be consequences. None of those truths helped them, however. Just as knowing that you are sinful or thinking God is mad at you does little for you even today. It is the realization that there is a way back that gives you the confidence and courage to get up and try again. The ability to approach God again is only made possible through the finished work of Jesus Christ on the Cross. Without it, victory and a way back to God would not be possible. Paul tells us in 1 Corinthians 2: 14, "Now thanks be to God who always leads us in triumph in Christ, and through us diffuses the fragrance of His knowledge in every place."

That is the "good news" of the Gospel! We do not have to live in defeat. We can shed the regimen of religious activity and know the victory that is available through a relationship with Jesus Christ. When Jesus was resurrected, he provided access to a victorious life for us. Colossians 2:13-15 tells us exactly what Jesus did for us.

And you, being dead in your trespasses and the uncircumcision of your flesh, He has made alive together with Him, having forgiven you all trespasses, having wiped out the handwriting of requirements that was against us, which was contrary to us. And He has taken it out of the way, having nailed it to the cross. Having disarmed principalities and powers, He made a public spectacle of them, triumphing over them in it.

Every enemy that will ever come against you was defeated by Jesus Christ. He is our Champion!

In 2014, I graduated from law school and sat for the bar exam. I had entered law school much later in life. I began the process at age 37 after an 11-year career as a teacher and assistant principal. A lot of things happened during my three years at law school. I buried my mother, went through some major family issues, started dating someone, and got engaged. As a matter of fact, I was planning a wedding, finishing up law school, and preparing for the bar exam simultaneously. If you know anything about the exam, and even if you don't, you can pretty much guess this was a bad idea. Though I tried to focus, there were so many other things going on in life that it did not get my full attention.

I sat for the exam anyway and waited patiently for my results. On announcement day I anxiously raced to the computer. I quickly scrolled to the M's. Adrienne Mayfield wasn't there. I missed the score by three points! If you have ever been disappointed, you know exactly how I felt. What you might not recognize that I immediately felt was embarrassment. Most of my classmates were celebrating. Their names were there. Mine wasn't. I would have to sit for the test again or walk away as a failure. Or at least that's what I thought. Not passing the exam brought a wave of emotions, fear, disappointment, and shock, but the one that refused to budge, even as I planned for my next attempt was feeling like a failure.

It was an almost daily struggle. My thoughts were my worst enemy. "You didn't pass. What's wrong with you! Everyone knows you didn't pass. All your classmates probably thought you were too old anyway. Guess you better go back to education. You just wasted your money." Although I pushed past it and eventually passed, even now I sometimes wonder what people will think when I say I didn't pass the first time.

Once I became a lawyer, I discussed my story with one of my mentors. She chided me, "Do not tell anyone else that. Ever. It doesn't matter." I considered her suggestion and shame even co-signed it, but I considered something else. What about all the other students who didn't pass the first time? If I never shared my story, they wouldn't be encouraged to know that they can pass the bar, too! Now, when I meet students who are preparing, I share my story. I don't let embarrassment silence me. People are encouraged to know that even after defeat, victory is possible.

Having a relationship with Christ does not mean that everything will always be perfect. It does not mean that we will never face difficulty or challenge in our lives. What it does mean is that whenever we face obstacles, we have someone who is going through the challenge with us, orchestrating a way to bring us to triumph. In addition, the victories we experience become a evidence of what He has done for us. Our story of overcoming encourages others to come to a saving relationship with Him too.

This promise gives us peace during adversity because when we obtain our victory, others will be strengthened and encouraged by our overcoming. We become "living epistles read of all men." 2 Corinthians 3:2. Suddenly, the sting of what we have endured begins to pale in comparison with the knowledge that our life has become a testament to others that they can be victorious as well. Please pray this prayer out loud with me.

Father, I thank you that you love me. I thank you that you are still undefeated! When I became a part of your family, I made a decision to win! I accept the blood of Jesus and the victory that His blood made possible for me. I will not think defeated. I will not live defeated. I will not act defeated. I will hold my head up high and remember that I am your child. Whenever I am tempted to forget, I will remind myself that you always cause me to triumph! Thank you for the victory in every area of my life. Amen.

CHAPTER 4

WE ARE WHOLE NOT BROKEN

A mosaic is a picture or pattern produced by arranging together small colored pieces of hard material, such as stone, tile, or glass. (Wikipedia). They are considered unique because of the variation of materials that can be used to create them. What begins as broken pieces becomes a masterpiece. Such is the case with our lives. We encounter challenges, struggles, and mishaps along the way. Any one of the experiences alone can be enough to make us quit or presume that we cannot make it, but somehow, when we are away from the event for a while, we begin to realize that it takes many different events to create the intricate stories of our lives.

Religion teaches us to lie about our brokenness. We are encouraged not to show weakness and pain. Living this way causes stress, high blood pressure, and other diseases. It is not healthy to hide your pain. Pain and brokenness signal our need for assistance. When we are broken, we are more open. This can be positive or negative, depending on how we deal with our feelings. If we open ourselves up to the wrong people, environments, or solutions when we are broken, we can end up even more damaged.

Brokenness is what causes many people to be introduced to the occult. When people are hurting, they get desperate. If it is a person who has wounded them, they often contemplate revenge. Some people experiment with magic so they can hurt the person who broke them. Others who are confused about their identity can get introduced to black magic, white magic, and voodoo in the same way. Satan capitalizes on the pain, rejection, and desperation and offers them what they perceive to be power and acceptance. It is not until they have made the deal that they realize they have compromised with a thief whose primary goal is to "steal, kill, and destroy." John 10:10.

Often it is not until we are broken that we realize that something exists that is bigger than we are. Sometimes is not until we have overcome a trial that we can begin to reasonably evaluate its implications. If we evaluate things properly, we can come out stronger and wiser than we were before. I've heard it said that what doesn't kill you makes you stronger, and I believe it's true. If you reach for God, He can help you make sense of the things that have happened in your life. Psalms 51:17 tells us, "The sacrifices of God *are* a broken spirit, A broken and a contrite heart— These, O God, You will not despise." When you develop a relationship with God, you can begin your journey toward wholeness. He deals with the cracks and wounds in your soul that have kept you broken and bruised.

Scripture tells us that God is near to the broken-hearted. That means you are never alone. Religion tells you that you can never touch God. It encourages you to seek performance instead of accepting that God can be known, experienced, and encountered just like your closest friend. Yet, in even the deepest times of hurt and loneliness, we have a Father who is with us. We need only call out to Him to feel the reassurance of His Presence. Scripture says in His presence is fullness of joy. That means that whenever we are sad, lonely, or broken, we can come into God's Presence and find all that we need to be healed, restored, and put back together.

Sometimes we experience so many hurts and disappointments that we think there is no hope. We often consider and have to admit that some of the issues we faced were actually of our own making. Because of that, we conclude that we deserve to be separated from God and punished for what we have done. The real truth is that when we accept Jesus as our personal Savior, all of our sins are covered—past, present, and future. We only have to confess them and ask Jesus to help us become more like Him. As we submit to the process, we begin to experience breakthrough and a discovery of who we were really created to be.

In Mark 5:23, Scripture tells us that a leader of the synagogue approached Jesus and told Him that his daughter had died. He followed by saying, but "if you will come lay hands on her, she will live." Jesus and the disciples got up to go with the man, but as they did, something else happened. All of a sudden, a woman in the crowd reached out and touched the fringes of His cloak. This was no ordinary woman. This was no fan seeking an autograph or her chance to get a selfie with "the next big thing." This woman actually had an issue. She needed help. She had been bleeding for over twelve years. She had gone to many doctors and spent all that she had. They were unable to heal her. Mark records that she said, "If I may only touch His clothes, I shall be made well."

One person approached Jesus boldly asking him to heal his daughter. The other simply crawled to Him to encounter His healing power. Both experienced the healing power of a Savior who knew and was sensitive to their plight. Jesus comes to make us whole.

In "Unchurched" by Todd Dulaney, the song tells a story of a person who has come to church searching for healing. The speaker says,

I heard that church was the place to come for my healing

but somehow I can't see how that's so

everyone seems to be so uneasy

maybe it's the way I look I'm unsure

If they give me the chance

I only want to make it to the altar to see the man

that's why I came today to change my ways

I am not ashamed

Many times people stay away from church because they feel their brokenness makes them unworthy. Sadly, when they do come, they are often treated unkindly. That should never be the case. Every one of us has a story, a past, and a destiny. No one is too dirty, too messed up, or too broken for God.

Jesus says to you today, "Come to Me, all you who labor and are heavy laden, and I will give you rest. Take My yoke upon you and learn from Me, for I am gentle and lowly in heart, and you will find rest for your souls. For My yoke is easy and My burden is light." Matthew 11:28-30. You are invited to bring your brokenness to Jesus so that He can make you whole. He promises rest for your soul. Soul rest means you can finally relax into who you were created to be, stop striving and just be.

This revelation is very freeing as it tells us that God doesn't require us to work or strive to please Him. If we come to Him with all that we are, He will accept us, embrace us, and give us the rest we need from working to achieve His love and affirmation. He affirms us and loves us already. We are created in His image. Please pray this prayer out loud with me.

Jesus, thank you for allowing yourself to be broken to win my wholeness. I accept the words that you spoke to the woman with the issue of blood as my very own. Today I declare that I will be made whole. My wholeness means there is nothing broken. There is nothing missing. Thank you so much. By an act of my will, I choose to forgive anyone who has ever hurt me, lied to me, betrayed me, or violated me. I release and forgive them now. (Pause and listen for any specific person or violation you need to forgive. Remember that God is your Father. He **can** and **will** talk to you.) In any area of my life where I have been broken, I ask you to repair it now. I ask you to inspect my heart. Any part that was broken, I ask that you fill the cracks with your love and

32

healing. You promised me peace so I ask that you would release it to me now. In Jesus' name. Amen.

CHAPTER 5

WE ARE FORGIVEN NOT ASHAMED

Merriam-Webster defines shame as a painful emotion caused by consciousness of guilt, shortcoming, or impropriety. Shame possesses the ability to completely debilitate an individual. It forces people into deep caves, depression, alienation, and can even push some people toward suicide. We've all felt it when we don't measure up to our own expectations or when someone makes us feel as if we don't measure up to theirs. Worse still is an awareness that we have done something that God likely would not approve of. While we should feel convicted when we sin, we should not be condemned. Condemnation does nothing but force us into reclusion.

I was raised in a small rural town in northeast Georgia. My family attended a small Baptist church every Sunday, and I learned most of the Bible characters I know from Sunday School. Although I'm sure it was not intentional, I always felt there was more discussion about God's punishment than his grace or love. I grew up in the 80's, so there was a very different cultural climate then than there is now. I remember the first time a young girl in our congregation became pregnant as if it were yesterday. There were murmurs, whispers, and horrified glances from the older women in the church. My father was a deacon, and my mom was a church administrator, so I was privy to some of their discussions.

One day, after church, I heard them recapping the events of Sunday service. My dad began to say, "I wonder when (the parents of the young girl) are planning to have her come forward to make her statement. "Her statement" was a standard in most Baptist churches in our town. If a young girl was pregnant without a husband, she was expected to come forward and express her shame and regret over the sin. They continued their discussion on the issue until I finally worked up my nerve to say something. "Dad, I don't understand. The girl did not get pregnant alone. Why is she the only one who has to come forward? What about the boy who got her pregnant? What about him?" He looked at me, puzzled, and said, " I guess because he doesn't go to church." While that was true, I doubted that was the real reason.

I knew some teenagers who were both in other churches. Even in those situations, only the young girl was expected to come forward to make "the statement." The young girl at our church eventually did come forward to apologize, and I remember feeling really embarrassed for her. I don't recall hearing about anyone talking to her privately, offering to disciple her, or finding a way to move her toward restoration. Inherently, I knew that being pregnant outside wedlock was a sin, yet I wondered if forcing her to make a public statement really changed anything other than to cloak her in shame.

The religious people of Jesus' day were no different. The Scribes and Pharisees were experts in Jewish law. Despite their knowledge of God and the law, Jesus rebuked them. One particular day, as Jesus concluded his teaching, they bring a woman before Him. The Bible records that she was a woman caught in the act of adultery. They said, "Teacher, this woman was caught in adultery, in the very act. Now Moses, in the law, commanded us that such should be stoned. But what do you say?" Jesus did not respond. Instead, he bent down and began writing on the ground. They persisted, so finally He responded. He raised Himself up and said, "He who is without sin among you, let him throw a stone at her first." He began writing again as the group, one by one, walked away. When only the woman and Jesus remained, he stood up and asked her who remained to accuse her. "No one, Lord." Jesus' response revealed His heart toward her. "Neither do I condemn you; go and sin no more." John 8:1-11.

Jesus' response was very different from the one many people receive today. He did not affirm her in sin for fear that she would be hurt or rejected or, worse yet, reject him. Neither did he pick up His own rock to join the crowd. Instead, He offered forgiveness and an admonition to go and sin no more. Jesus' understood what those in many religious circles do not. When an individual truly comes face-to-face with the mercy and grace of God, the heart can be shaped. The gratitude that comes from love and acceptance can move an individual to make lasting change—change that comes from relationship, not religion.

To receive forgiveness, when we know we have sinned, should not create license to sin; but rather, a determination to live for the one who has granted the forgiveness. Therefore, the fear many have about teaching the totality of the Gospel, which is salvation received by faith through grace, is unfounded. Receiving true love makes one love more, not less. The forgiveness we receive when we accept Jesus as our Savior means we exchange our shame for His acceptance.

"If we confess our sins, He is faithful to forgive us our sins and cleanse us from all righteousness." I John 1:9. Having a relationship with Jesus puts us in right standing with God. Many pastors fear preaching on the grace of God for fear that individuals will use the grace of God to excuse sin. Nothing can be further from the truth. Whenever you get a real grasp of the grace of God and what it cost to reconcile you back to Him, you will never consider grace as cheap or casual. Jesus' blood was shed to make it possible for us to have a relationship with God. He hung on a cross, naked, with nails in His hand and feet so that our sins could be paid for. There is nothing about that truth that should ever make you believe it was not costly.

Jesus left the beauty and grandeur of Heaven to come to Earth, live a sinless life where he was misunderstood, rejected, and crucified, all so you could know Him and have a relationship with the Father. His sacrifice means we do not have to fear the condemnation of an angry Father. Rather, we are accepted into the family of God. When we sin, we need only confess, repent (which means we agree with God that our behavior was sin and turn away from it), and seek the guidance of Holy Spirit to walk forward. From there, we trust the Holy Spirit to teach and train us how to look and live like Jesus. That is actually why Holy Spirit and Jesus switched places. Jesus went back to Heaven, and Holy Spirit came to Earth to live inside every believer. When Jesus was preparing for His return to Heaven, He told the disciples, "The Helper, the Holy Spirit, whom the Father will send in My name, He will teach you all things, and bring to your remembrance all things that I said to you." John 14:26.

Once we accept Jesus and partner with Holy Spirit, we no longer need to walk in shame and condemnation. We live in our identity as children of God. When God sees us, He sees us through the eyes of Jesus which means that we are loved, accepted, and forgiven. Now that's good news! While religion will tell you that you must hide away from a God who could never accept you, Jesus invites you into a relationship with Him where you can experience forgiveness, fellowship, and the love of a Father who created you just so He could fellowship with you. If you have never asked Jesus to come live in your heart, please pray this prayer out loud with me.

Father, I confess that I am a sinner. I thank you for the blood of Jesus. I repent for the ways I have sinned against you and grieved your heart. Today, I choose by an act of my will to accept your sacrifice on my behalf. I believe that Jesus was born of a virgin, crucified, and raised on the third day. I ask you now to come into my life as Savior and Lord. I will not cling to religion. I will seek a growing relationship with you. Thank you that I no longer wear a cloak of shame. I am forgiven, and I thank you for this gift. I did nothing to earn it. I receive it by faith. Amen.

If you prayed that prayer for the first time, please be sure to drop me a note. Welcome to the family of God! If you are already a believer, but have never received the baptism of Holy Spirit, please pray this prayer aloud with me now:

Holy Spirit, I believe that you are the third member of the Trinity. You are not a force, a wind, or a thing. You are a person. Thank you for coming to Earth to teach me, to train me, and to reveal all Truth. I ask you now to come and live inside me. Fill me with yourself. I will not be ashamed of you, your gifts, or the supernatural power you give me. I invite you to pray through me with my own unique prayer language. Convey what I cannot and pray the perfect will of the Father for my life. I receive you now, by faith in Jesus' name. Amen.

CHAPTER 6

WE ARE ACCEPTED NOT REJECTED

I doubt there is anyone alive who has not experienced the agonizing fear that accompanies playground games that are made of teams. I don't have to think very hard myself to remember the tension and prayers that came with waiting to be chosen. Though the choices were often made on the basis of skill, many times, choices were based on popularity alone. I was almost 5'11 when I was in 4th grade, so I never had to wait very long to be chosen for the basketball pick-up games. When something required racing, though, that was altogether different. Though I had long legs, I never really ran that fast, and all the kids knew it. When it was time for teams to be chosen for racing . . .well, let's just say I was not a first-round draft pick.

I hadn't really thought much about those childhood games until I began writing, but as I type, I can vividly remember the emotions I felt when I was not picked. I also remember crying once in P.E. because I was deathly afraid of having to dribble the ball full court and shoot a lay-up. I knew if I missed, the other kids would make fun of me, and I might not be chosen for teams.

Rejection is real, and it is painful. Rejection from grade school buddies is one thing, but to be rejected by your family is something much worse. Consider the story of Joseph in Genesis 37.

Joseph and his 11 brothers were the sons of Jacob. Jacob (Israel) "played favorites" with his children, and it had disastrous results. "Now, Israel loved Joseph more than all his children, because he was the son of his old age. Also, he made him a tunic of many colors. But when his brothers saw that their father loved him more than all his brothers, they hated him and could not speak peaceably to him." Genesis 37:3-4. Not only did Jacob have a favorite child, he made it obvious to his children by giving Joseph a special coat. As expected, his brothers became resentful and hated their brother. One day Joseph had a dream. He dreamt about binding sheaves with his brothers. Suddenly, his sheaf rose and his brothers' sheaves stood around his sheaf and bowed. Joseph decided to share his dream with his brothers, and their response is not at all surprising. "And his brothers said to him, Shall you indeed reign over us? Or shall you indeed have dominion over us?' So they hated him even more for his dreams and for his words." v. 8.

Later, Joseph had another dream and shared it, as well. This time, the dream seemed to convey that one day, his entire family would bow to him. His father rebuked him, "What is this dream that you have dreamed? Shall your mother and I and your brothers indeed come to bow down to the earth before you? And his brothers envied him, but his father kept the matter in mind." v. 10-11.

One day, Joseph's father sent him to go to check on his brothers who were away, feeding the flock. Joseph's brothers saw him before he saw them, and they were not happy. "Now when they saw him afar off, even before he came near them, they conspired against him to kill him. Then they said to one another, "Look, this dreamer is coming! Come, therefore, let us now kill him and cast him into some pit; and we shall say, 'Some wild beast has devoured him.' We shall see what will become of his dreams!" v. 18-20. They had not forgotten his dream, and they wanted to ensure that it had no chance to come to fruition.

One brother, Reuben, talked them into putting him in a pit, instead, so he could attempt a rescue later. These were Joseph's brothers. Not strangers, but his very own brothers.

Joseph was oblivious to their plan. When he reached them, they stripped his coat and threw him into a pit. Then, they sat down to eat a meal! The story does have a happy ending, read Genesis 37-47 to read the entire story, but not before Joseph got to become the poster child for rejection.

Jesus was rejected, too. He was rejected in His hometown. In fact, though He was performing miracles everywhere else, Scripture tells us he could do very few miracles there. He was rejected as He hung on a Cross for you and me, so now we do not have to live with the sting of rejection. He overcame it, so we could walk in victory. Even if people shun you, alienate you, or leave you out, you are never rejected. God says, "You are mine."

Religion may tell you that you don't fit. It may even tell you that you don't belong. It may lie to you and say that God can never forgive you or want you after the things you have done. Do not believe the lie. The blood of Jesus makes all things possible. You can be reconciled to God. There are no rules to get to Jesus. You simply accept Him by faith. From there, you must believe that you are a part of God's family. Please pray this prayer out loud with me.

Father, I choose to believe that I am a part of your family. You love me, and I am created in your image. Even if men reject me or do not understand me, that is not my identity. I am accepted in the Beloved. I am chosen. I belong to you. Jesus, you promised never to leave me or forsake me. I stand on the Truth of that promise. You are with me. I am never alone. Heal my heart of any cracks that have come from people who have rejected me. I choose to forgive them. I will say like Jesus, "Father, forgive them, because they do not know what they are doing." Heal their hearts, as well. Thank you for loving me. Amen.

CHAPTER 7

WE ARE DEMONSTRATORS NOT TALKERS

Do you believe in miracles? When was the last time you experienced one? I don't mean watching YouTube, Facebook, or television. I mean a real, live miracle. Chances are you haven't seen one in a while. Why is that, exactly? Jesus performed many miracles during his time on Earth and told his disciples that they would do even "greater works." I believe one of the primary hindrances to the release of miracles in our modern world is the spirit of religion.

Religion attempts to keep our focus on what we can do in our own strength. Religion restricts the movement and activity of Holy Spirit, and often religion tells us, "It doesn't really take all that." When we limit the freedom of God's Spirit, we are less likely to experience any aspect of the supernatural.

I have never seen a dead man raised, but I have seen a miracle firsthand. One day I was speaking at a church when I noticed a lady seated in the middle of the row. Something kept drawing my attention to her, so I called her up front. Immediately, I sensed my hands getting warmer so I knew Holy Spirit was giving me His power to heal. Without any description of what ailed her, I bent down and started praying for her knee. My hands felt hot as fire, and I could feel the heat radiating into her tissues. I said a prayer, not feeling as if I needed to say very much, as the miracle was already taking place.

She started laughing, crying, and screaming at the same time. "The Lord healed me! The Lord healed me! How did you know?" She was shocked that God had chosen to heal her without making a request. I had no way of knowing that her knee was hurt, except by the knowledge of God.

I know there will be naysayers who read this story and doubt its validity, and that's okay. God does not have low self-esteem! He is more than able to prove the validity of His power anytime. Anywhere. With all the emphasis on the paranormal, demons, witchcraft, and magic, it always surprises me that people question the existence of the supernatural. I actually think it might be more of an issue in religious circles than anywhere else. Ask any child or teenager about Harry Potter, the use of sage, or a séance, and you will likely be surprised. They are well versed on these things. There is an interest in the supernatural, the emphasis just seems to be more on the powers of darkness than light. This must change. We, as believers in Jesus Christ, have the real power.

Powers of darkness have always tried to pretend they have more power than God. The magicians were able to make their staffs turn into snakes just like Moses did, but Moses' snake ate theirs! Satan, whose name was Lucifer before he was kicked out of heaven even tried to challenge God. He was so cunning that he was able to convince 1/3 of the angels in heaven to join him! It mattered little though. Jesus said, "and I saw Lucifier fall like lightning from heaven." Like heaven! God doesn't play around. There is another famous show-down in the Bible where God demonstrates his power—the story of Elijah and the prophets of Baal. The children of Israel had begun worship of the idol Baal. Elijah confronted them and proposed a challenge to demonstrate which god was real. Then Elijah said to the people,

"I alone am left a prophet of the Lord; but Baal's prophets are four hundred and fifty men. Therefore let them give us two bulls; and let them choose one bull for themselves, cut it in pieces, and lay it on the wood, but put no fire under it; and I will prepare the other bull, and lay it on the wood, but put no fire under it. Then you call on the name of your gods, and I will call on the name of the Lord; and the God who answers by fire, He is God. 1 Kings 18:22-24

Baal's prophets prepared their bull, called on Baal from the morning to noon, but nothing happened. Elijah mocked them, suggesting maybe they should shout louder, suggesting that perhaps their god was talking, sleeping or on vacation! They jumped on the altar and cut themselves. Still, there was no answer. Then they prophesied. Still— nothing. Finally, it was Elijah's turn. He added a little something extra so there would be no doubt— water!

He repaired the altar of the LORD that was broken down. And Elijah took twelve stones, according to the number of the tribes of the sons of Jacob, to whom the word of the LORD had come, saying, "Israel shall be your name." Then with the stones he built an altar in the name of the LORD; and he made a trench around the altar large enough to hold two seahs of seed. And he put the wood in order, cut the bull in pieces, and laid it on the wood, and said, "Fill four water pots with water, and pour it on the burnt sacrifice and on the wood." Then he said, "Do it a second time," and they did it a second time; and he said, "Do it a third time," and they did it a third time. So the water ran all around the altar; and he also filled the trench with water. v. 30-35

Elijah prayed to God, and "the fire of the LORD fell and consumed the burnt sacrifice, and the wood and the stones and the dust, and it licked up the water that *was* in the trench." v.38. He is the only God who could answer by fire. God proved that He is the only true God. There is no other God who is more powerful than Him. Still, He is the God who offers Himself to you. He is the God who reaches out for you today to show you how much He loves you. You can do more than talk about His power because He is the God who gives you the power to demonstrate who He is.

There is no reason why the Church should have a sick and shut in list with 50 people on it. James gives the Biblical prescription for sickness. "Is anyone among you sick? Let him call for the elders of the church, and let them pray over him, anointing him with oil in the name of the Lord. And the prayer of faith will save the sick, and the Lord will raise him up." James 5:14-15. We must begin to do the things that Jesus did so that we can begin to change the world. Please pray this prayer aloud with me.

Father, thank you for the gift of the Holy Spirit. Thank you that He gives me the power to live a victorious life and communicate with you. Forgive me for the times when I have shied away from praying for someone because I doubted your ability or willingness to heal. I ask now that you will give me courage and boldness that I might stand for your righteousness and I will be ready to speak or act whenever you prompt me. Remind me that all good gifts come from you. Because of you, I have power to overcome the enemy and teach others to do the same. Use me to do great miracles that point people back to you. In Jesus' name. Amen.

CONCLUSION

We have not yet seen the Church's finest hour. There is a remnant rising with power, truth, and the knowledge of all God has called us to be. We will not be bound by the spirit of religion. We will contend for authentic relationship with God. May you be counted among this great company who will join Jesus Christ in His return. As you complete this book, I pray this prayer over you.

My prayer is that you have new vitality for the Body of Christ and a renewed passion for the Father and His Word. I pray that you will experience the authentic relationship that is only available through a relationship with Jesus Christ. I curse every religious spirit that would seek to keep you in bondage to works instead of faith. I pray that you will walk in the freedom that comes from knowing that you are a son of God and not a slave. I pray that you will walk in the victory that is yours because of the finished work of Jesus Christ on the Cross. May you never know defeat.

I pray that you will be made whole, in your spirit, soul, mind, and body. I release healing to every part of your personality, identity, heart, and body. Father, remind them that they are forgiven through the blood of Jesus. May they never walk in the condemnation that makes them afraid to come into your Presence. I break every cloak of shame that has come over their lives for mistakes of the past. I thank you that they walk in the power and demonstration of your Holy Spirit to transform their lives and the lives of those in their sphere of influence. May any weariness, hurt, or disappointment they have had from the Church be broken from their lives. I pray that you will give them a fresh touch of your Holy Spirit that will be a tangible reminder of your love for them. Bless them, Father, keep them. May your countenance shine forth upon them. I pray that you will be gracious to them. Make your face turn toward them and give them peace. In Jesus' name. Amen.

Do you feel stuck?

Can't seem to figure out your next move?

Allow Me to Help You Unlock your Destiny!

Visit **adriennemayfield.com** and sign up for your personalized purpose coaching session today.

Do you have a story to tell?

Could others benefit from your history?

Do you journal, write poetry, or short stories?

Have you ever thought about writing a book?

Allow  **to put**

Visit adriennemayfield.com and place your interest inquiry in the Contact Me box today!